Teach Me...™
Everyday
ENGLISH
Volume 2
Celebrating the Seasons

Written by Judy Mahoney
Illustrated by Patrick Girouard

Our mission at Teach Me... to enrich children through language learning.

The *Teach Me Everyday* series of books introduces common words, phrases and concepts to the beginning language learner through delightful songs and story. These engaging books are designed with an audio CD, encouraging children to read, listen and speak. *Teach Me Everyday Volume 2* celebrates the seasons and activities throughout the year. Follow Marie and her family as they venture out to the zoo, go on a picnic, visit museums, build a snowman and celebrate the holidays. The audio is narrated in English and introduces music memory through familiar songs. Children of all ages will enjoy exploring new languages as they sing and learn with *Teach Me*.

The English language developed mainly from the Anglo-Saxon and Norman-French languages. Today, English is the most widely spoken language in the world. In many countries, it is either the native language or a secondary language. Over 350 million people speak English as their native language. It has a very large vocabulary with over 600,000 words, with new words being added every year.

Teach Me Everyday English – Volume 2: Celebrating the Seasons
ISBN 13: 978-1-59972-208-5 (library binding)
Library of Congress Control Number: 2008902655

Copyright © 2009 by Teach Me Tapes Inc.
6016 Blue Circle Drive, Minnetonka, MN 55343 USA
www.teachmeinc.com

Book design by Design Lab, Northfield, Minnesota.
Compact discs are replicated in the United States of America in Maple Grove, Minnesota.

Printed in the United States of America in North Mankato, Minnesota.
092009
08212009

10 9 8 7 6 5 4 3 2

INDEX & SONG LIST

SPRING

SUMMER

FALL

WINTER

You'll Sing a Song
You'll sing a song and I'll sing a song
And we'll sing a song together
You'll sing a song and I'll sing a song
In warm or wintry weather.

Hello! My name is Marie.
This is my brother. His name is Peter.
We have a dog. His name is Spot.
We have a cat. Her name is Fluffy.
Follow us through the year.
umbrella
rain
boots
five

I plant seeds to grow fruit and vegetables in my garden. This year, I will grow strawberries, tomatoes, carrots, cabbage and pumpkins.

garden

Oats and Beans and Barley Grow

Oats and beans and barley grow
Oats and beans and barley grow
Do you or I or anyone know
How oats and beans and barley grow?

First the farmer plants the seeds
Stands up tall and takes his ease
Stamps his feet and claps his hands
And turns around to view his land.

Then the farmer waters the ground
Watches the sun shine all around
Stamps his feet and claps his hands
And turns around to view his land.

carrots

giraffe

monkey

donkey

lion

Going to the Zoo

Momma's taking us to the zoo tomorrow
Zoo tomorrow, zoo tomorrow
Momma's taking us to the zoo tomorrow
We can stay all day.

We're going to the zoo, zoo, zoo
How about you, you, you?
You can come too, too, too
We're going to the zoo, zoo, zoo.

Look at all the monkeys swingin' in the trees...
Look at all the crocodiles swimmin' in the water...

Tingalayo

Tingalayo, come little donkey come
Tingalayo, come little donkey come
Me donkey fast, me donkey slow
Me donkey come and me donkey go
Me donkey fast, me donkey slow
Me donkey come and me donkey go.

Tingalayo, come little donkey come
Tingalayo, come little donkey come
Me donkey hee, me donkey haw
Me donkey sleep in a bed of straw
Me donkey dance, me donkey sing
Me donkey wearing a diamond ring.

OK. Now it's time to play Simon Says!

Simon Says Game

Simon says: "Put your right hand on your head!"

Simon says: "Touch the ground!"

Simon says: "Walk!"

Simon says: "Clap your hands!"

Simon says: "Say your name!"

"Laugh out loud." "Simon didn't say!"

dog

eleven

11

boat

ball

Sailing, Sailing
Sailing, sailing
Over the bounding main
For many a stormy wind shall blow
'Til Jack comes home again.

Row, Row, Row Your Boat
Row, row, row your boat
Gently down the stream
Merrily, merrily, merrily, merrily
Life is but a dream.

Down by the Seashore
Down by the seashore, watch the little sea gulls
As they waddle down the beach, all in a row
Down by the seashore, see the little tug boats
Pulling all the oil tankers, all in a row
Down by the seashore, see the little sailboats
As they glide across the waves, all in a row.

Down by the seashore, see the little girls
As they build their sand castles, all in a row
Down by the seashore, see the little boys
As they race their toy boats, all in a row
Down by the seashore, see the sun is setting
Watch the people as they leave, all in a row.

After our picnic, we go for a walk.

ocean

Things of the Ocean

Little drops of water, little grains of sand
Make the mighty ocean so beautiful and grand
Little bubbles floating, little snails that slide
Make the mighty ocean so beautiful and grand.

Every fish and coral, every bird and clam
Make the mighty ocean so beautiful and grand
Every weed and turtle, every whale and crab
Make the mighty ocean so beautiful and grand.

Gentle dolphins swimming, gentle rolling waves
Make the mighty ocean so beautiful and grand
Gentle gliding pelicans, a gentle seal at rest
Make the mighty ocean so beautiful and grand.

All the tiny sea shells, all the tiny bugs
Make the mighty ocean so beautiful and grand
All the tiny treasures, on the tiny islands
Make the mighty ocean so beautiful and grand.

Next, we go across the street to visit the art museum.

I like to look at the bulls in Goya's painting. I pretend I am the matador.

Look at the painting by Van Gogh! The flowers in his painting look like the ones in my garden.

White Coral Bells
White coral bells upon a slender stalk
Lilies of the valley deck our garden walk
Oh, don't you wish that you could hear them ring?
That can happen only when the fairies sing.

September

tree

cat

leaf

rake

The Green Grass Grew

There was a tree
In all the woods
The prettiest tree
That you ever did see.

The tree in the hole
And the hole in the ground
The green grass grew all around,
    all around
And the green grass grew
    all around.

And on that tree...
There was limb...

And on that limb...
There was a branch...

And on that branch...
There was a twig...

And on that twig...
There was an acorn...

And by that acorn...
There was a leaf...

The leaf by the acorn
And the acorn on the twig
And the twig on the branch
And the branch on the limb
And the limb on the tree
And the tree in the hole
And the hole in the ground
The green grass grew all around,
    all around
And the green grass grew
    all around.

After summer, it is autumn. The leaves turn gold, red and orange. We gather leaves and acorns that fall from the trees.

squirrel

acorns

grandpa

corn

Before we go back to school, we visit Grandpa's farm. We feed the cows, chickens and pigs.

Grandpa shears the wool from the sheep. Later, he takes us on a hayride with our cousins.

Down on Grandpa's Farm

Oh, we're on our way, we're on our way
On our way to Grandpa's farm
We're on our way, we're on our way
On our way to Grandpa's farm.

Down on Grandpa's farm there is a big brown cow
Down on Grandpa's farm there is a big brown cow
The cow, she makes a sound like this: Moo!
The cow, she makes a sound like this: Moo!

Down on Grandpa's farm, there is a little red hen
Down on Grandpa's farm, there is a little red hen
The hen, she makes a sound like this: Cluck! Cluck!
The hen, she makes a sound like this: Cluck! Cluck!

sheep

Baa Baa Black Sheep

Baa baa black sheep, have you any wool?
Yes Sir, yes Sir, three bags full
One for my master and one for my dame
One for the little boy who lives down the lane
Baa baa black sheep, have you any wool?
Yes Sir, yes Sir, three bags full.

chickens

cow

Old MacDonald

Old MacDonald had a farm, E - I - E - I - O
And on that farm he had a cow, E - I - E - I - O
With a moo, moo here and a moo, moo there
Here a moo, there a moo, everywhere a moo, moo
Old MacDonald had a farm, E - I - E - I - O.

And on that farm he had a chicken, E - I - E - I - O
With a cluck, cluck here and a cluck, cluck there...

And on that farm he had a cat, E - I - E - I – O
With a meow, meow here and a meow, meow there...

And on that farm he had some sheep, E - I - E - I – O
With a baa, baa here and a baa, baa there...

October

It is Halloween. I am carving a face on my pumpkin.

pumpkin

Five Little Pumpkins
Five little pumpkins sitting on a gate.
The first one said, "Oh my, it's getting late."
The second one said, "There are witches in the air."
The third one said, "But we don't care."
The fourth one said, "Let's run and run and run."
The fifth one said, "I'm ready for some fun."
"Oo-oo," went the wind and out went the light
And the five little pumpkins rolled out of sight.

moon

owl

Tonight, I will dress up in my Little Red Riding Hood costume and Spot will be the wolf. Peter will be a cowboy. Then we will go trick-or-treating with our friends.

November

fair

After Halloween it is November.

Today, our parents take us to the fall festival. We bring the vegetables from our garden to be judged.

There are many rides for the children. I love to ride the merry-go-round.

horse

America the Beautiful
Oh beautiful for spacious skies
For amber waves of grain
For purple mountain majesties
Above the fruited plain
America, America
God shed His grace on thee
And crown thy good with brotherhood
From sea to shining sea.

December

snow

Look, snow is falling! Let's go and play in the snow. We take our sleds and slide down the hill.

Then we'll build a huge snowman. He has coal eyes, a carrot nose and a derby hat. He wears my mother's scarf.

snowman

Snowman Song

There's a friend of mine
You might know him, too
Wears a derby hat
He's real cool.

He has coal black eyes
An orange carrot nose
Two funny stick-like arms
And a snowy overcoat.

Have you guessed his name
Or do you need a clue?
You'll never see his face
In autumn, summer, spring.

Who is it?
Can you guess?
C'mon, guess!
C'mon, don't you know?
It's the snowman!

Jingle Bells

Jingle bells, jingle bells
Jingle all the way
Oh what fun it is to ride
In a one-horse open sleigh, hey!

Dashing through the snow
In a one-horse open sleigh
O'er the fields we go
Laughing all the way
Bells on bob-tails ring
Making spirits bright
What fun it is to laugh and sing
A sleighing song tonight!

Silent Night

Silent night, holy night
All is calm, all is bright
'Round yon Virgin, Mother and Child
Holy infant, so tender and mild
Sleep in heavenly peace
Sleep in heavenly peace.

It is holiday time.
We celebrate Christmas.
We bake cookies and decorate
our house. We sing
special songs.

cookies

January

HAPPY NEW

balloon

YEAR!

January first begins the new year. We have a party to celebrate on New Year's Eve.

Auld Lang Syne
Should auld acquaintance be forgot
And never brought to mind?
Should auld acquaintance be forgot
And days of auld lang syne?

For auld lang syne, my dear
For auld lang syne
We'll take a cup of kindness yet
For auld lang syne!

February

beads

mask

In February, we celebrate the Mardi Gras carnival. It is fun. I like to catch candy at the parade. We wear costumes and sing and dance with our friends.

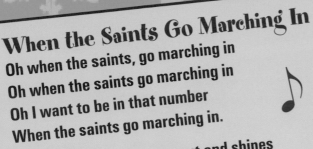

When the Saints Go Marching In

Oh when the saints, go marching in
Oh when the saints go marching in
Oh I want to be in that number
When the saints go marching in.

Oh when the sun, comes out and shines
Oh when the sun comes out and shines
I want to be in that number
When the sun comes out and shines.
Yeah!

Now we know the months of the year. Do you?

January
February
March
April
May
June
July
August
September
October
November
December

What a fun year!

January

February

March

April

May

June

July

August

September

October

November

December